KU-309-063

To the boy behind the door - K.G.

For Laura, Grace and Oscar - L.W.

BOLTON LIBRARIES	
18086314	
Bertrams	30/08/2011
	£10.99
LL	

First published in 2011 by Hodder Children's Books

Text copyright © Kes Gray 2011
Illustrations copyright © Lee Wildish 2011

Hodder Children's Books, 338 Euston Road, London, NW1 3BH
Hodder Children's Books Australia, Level 17/207 Kent Street, Sydney, NSW 2000

The right of Kes Gray and Lee Wildish to be identified as the author
and illustrator of this Work has been asserted by them in accordance
with the Copyright, Designs and Patents Act 1988.

All rights reserved.
A catalogue record of this book is available from the British Library.
ISBN 978 1 444 90014 9
10 9 8 7 6 5 4 3 2 1

Printed in China
Hodder Children's Books is a division of Hachette Children's Books,
an Hachette UK Company

www.hachette.co.uk

Leave me Alone

Kes  **Gray**

Illustrated by Lee Wildish

Hodder Children's Books

A division of Hachette Children's Books

'Leave me alone,' I said.

'Sorry,' said the fly.
'I saw you looking miserable,
And couldn't pass you by.'

'Leave me alone,' I said.
'Sorry,' said the frog.
'You're looking so downhearted,
I had to leave my log.'

'Leave me alone,' I said.
'Sorry,' said the robin.
'Pardon me for asking,
But did I hear you sobbing?'

'Leave me alone,' I said.

'Sorry,' said the cat.

'Your sadness makes my whiskers wilt,

I think we need to chat.'

'Leave me alone,' I said.

'Sorry,' said the rabbit.

'Helping people who need help

Has always been a habit.'

'Leave me alone,' I said.
'Sorry,' said the cow.
'I'd like to cheer you up as well,
But need to find out how.'

'Leave me alone,' I said.
'Sorry,' said Magpie.
'I see that you're unhappy,
What I need to see is why.'

'Leave me alone,' I said.
'Sorry,' said the pig.
'But problems should be talked about,
Especially if they're big.'

'Leave me alone,' I said.
'They're far too big for you.
They're far too big for anyone,
There's nothing you can do.

My problem is a giant
So big he blocks the sun,
Who teases me and bullies me
Every day for fun.

A giant full of nasty words,
A giant huge and strong,
Who casts a shadow over me
That's kilometres long.

There's nothing you can do for me,
There's nothing you can say.
Oh no, the ground is shaking!
He's heading right this way!'

ALONE!'

they said; the rabbit and the fly,
the cow, the frog, the pig,
the cat, the robin
and Magpie.

I shut my eyes, then opened them.
Not one voice, two or three,
But eight loud voices all at once
Were standing up for me!

Tall as mighty tree trunks,
Brave as brave can be,
My friends stood tall, and strong and firm
And faced my enemy.

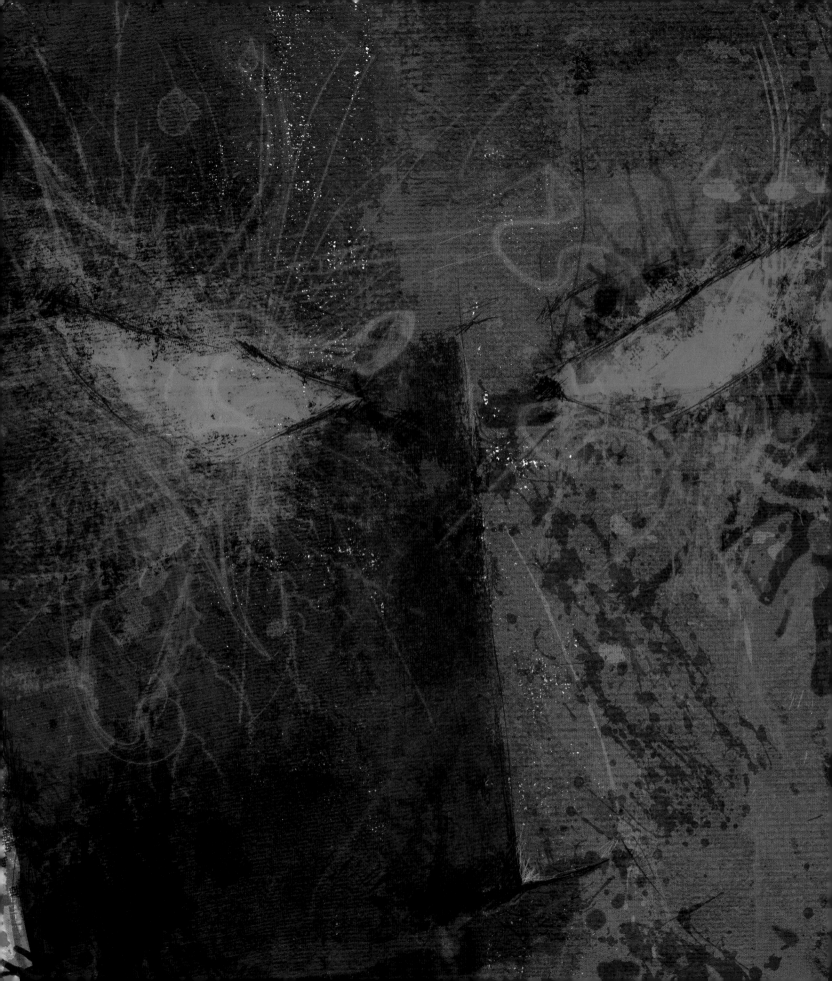

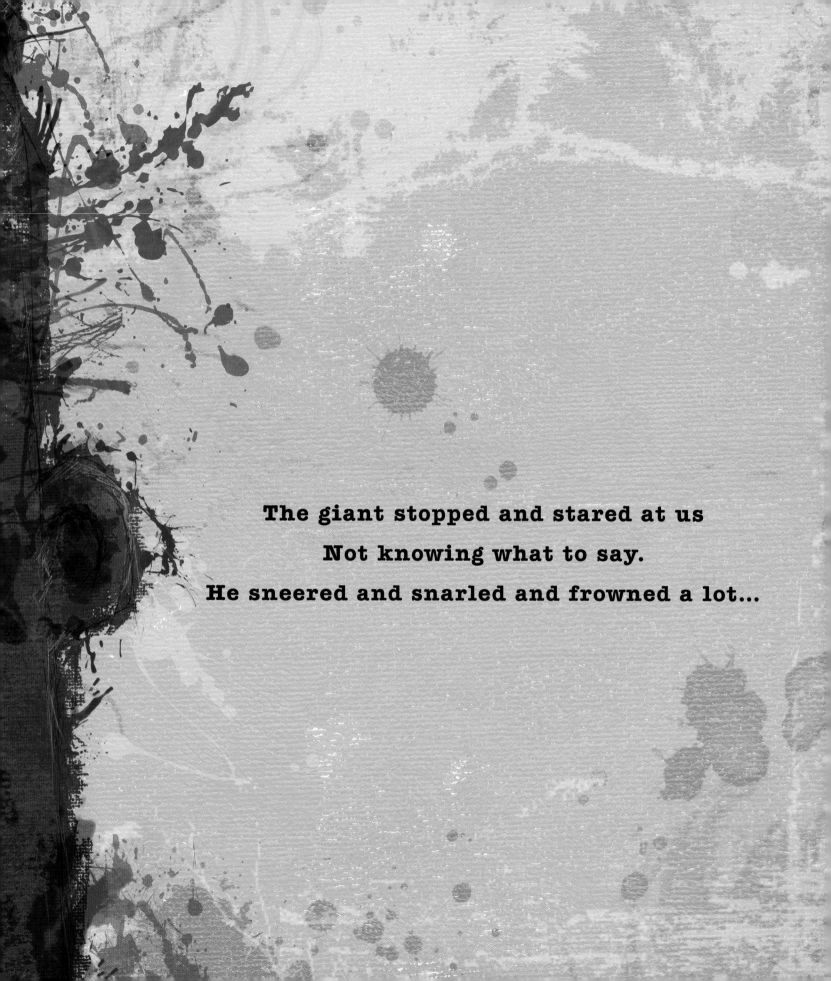

The giant stopped and stared at us
Not knowing what to say.
He sneered and snarled and frowned a lot...

And then he walked away!

He took his dark, dark shadow
And stomped across the hill.

I never saw him after that
And I know I never will.

the End